the baby who wouldn't go to bed

For
Caledonia

With thanks to
Ian Butterworth,
Annie Eaton
and Ted Dewan

TRANSWORLD PUBLISHERS LTD
61-63 Uxbridge Road, London W5 5SA

TRANSWORLD PUBLISHERS (AUSTRALIA) PTY LTD
15-25 Helles Avenue, Moorebank, NSW 2170

TRANSWORLD PUBLISHERS (NZ) LTD
3 William Pickering Drive, Albany, Auckland

DOUBLEDAY CANADA LTD
105 Bond Street, Toronto, Ontario M5B 1Y3

Published in 1996 by Doubleday
a division of Transworld Publishers Ltd
Reprinted 1997 (twice)

Copyright © 1996 by Helen Cooper

This edition produced for
The Book People Ltd,
Hall Wood Avenue,
Haydock,
St Helens WA11 9UL

The right of Helen Cooper to be identified as the Author
of this work has been asserted in accordance with
the Copyright, Designs and Patents Act 1988
A catalogue record for this book is available
from the British Library

ISBN 0385 408668

Printed in Belgium by Proost

the baby who wouldn't go to bed

Pictures and Story by
Helen Cooper

TED SMART

"Bedtime!"
said the Mother.

"No!"
said the Baby,
playing in his car.
"It's still light."

"But it's summer,"
said the Mother.

A little bit later...

"Bedtime!"
said the Mother.

"NO!"
said the Baby,
playing in his car.
"I'm going to stay up
all night."

"Oh, no you're not!"
said the Mother.

But the Baby revved up his car
...vrrruuum-chugga-chug...
then drove away
as fast as he could,
and the Mother couldn't
catch him.

Well, he hadn't driven very
far before he met a tiger.
"Let's play at roaring,"
said the Baby.

But the tiger was too tired.
"Night time is for snoring,
not roaring,"
yawned the tiger.
"Come back in the morning,
I'll play with you then."

So off went the Baby…
vrrruuum-chugga-chug
…till he met a troop
of soldiers.

"Let's march," said the
Baby. But the soldiers
were too sleepy.

"Night time is for
dreaming, not
parading," said the
captain.
"We're going back to
our castle. And so
should you."

Sleepytown

Awakeville

Castl...

But the Baby didn't want to. He trundled away in his car...

...vrrruuum-chugga-chug

...as fast as he could.

Next he came across a little train.
"Race you to the station for
a jolly good smash-up," said the Baby.

But the train was too tired.

"Night time is for resting, not racing," said the train.

"I'm going home to my depot, and so should you."

But still the Baby rumbled along the road… vrrruuum-chugga-chug… till he met some musicians.

"Let's have a party and dance all night," said the Baby.

But the musicians were too drowsy. "We're really, really tired," they said. "But give us a lift home, and we'll play you a lullaby instead."

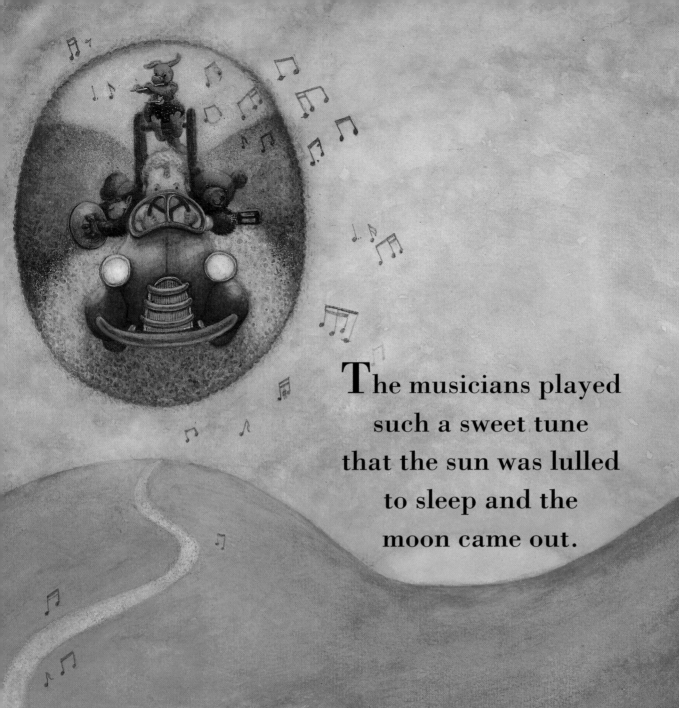

The musicians played
such a sweet tune
that the sun was lulled
to sleep and the
moon came out.

The little car went slower...

and slower...

and slower...

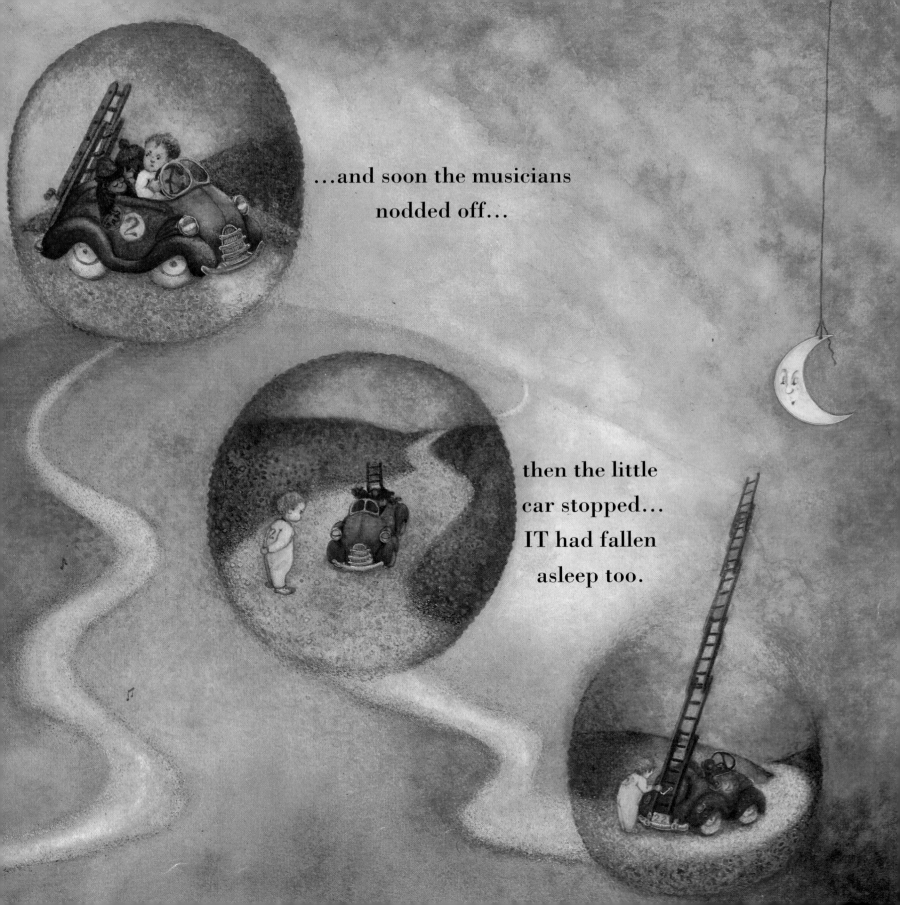

...and soon the musicians
nodded off...

then the little
car stopped...
IT had fallen
asleep too.

The Baby looked up at
the moon.
"Can't we have a midnight
feast?" he wailed.

"It's bedtime,"
sighed the moon drowsily.

And even the moon
closed her eyes and dozed off.

Now the Baby had to
push the car
in the dusky dark.

It was hard work.

And soon he'd gone as far as he could.
So he stood quite still, all alone,
with the sleeping world around him.

But there was someone else who was not asleep.
Someone who was looking for the Baby…

and getting nearer…

and nearer…

and nearer…
all the time.

Someone who was ever so weary,
but couldn't go to bed until the Baby did.

It was the Mother.
And the Baby hugged her.

Then the Mother lifted up the Baby with one arm, and pushed the car with the other...
(She was a very strong Mother.)

And she trundled and bundled them
all the way home.

"Bedtime?"
said the Baby sleepily.
"No," whispered the Mother.
"You said you were
staying up
all night!"

"**Y**-a-w-n,"
said the Baby.

"Alright then,"
said the Mother.

"Good night."